For Esme, a true citizen of the world!

Dear Reader,
This is a picture of my little friend Esme
and her family. Esme was born in China,
but her mom is Welsh and English
and her dad is Indian. Lucky Esme —
she has a toe in four different countries!
This book is to remind Esme of her
Indian family and friends and to give
you a chance to take a walk through
India with some of its fantastic animals.
Namaste,
Marcia

The Elephant's Friend
and
Other Tales
from
Ancient India

retold and illustrated by
Marcia Williams

CANDLEWICK PRESS

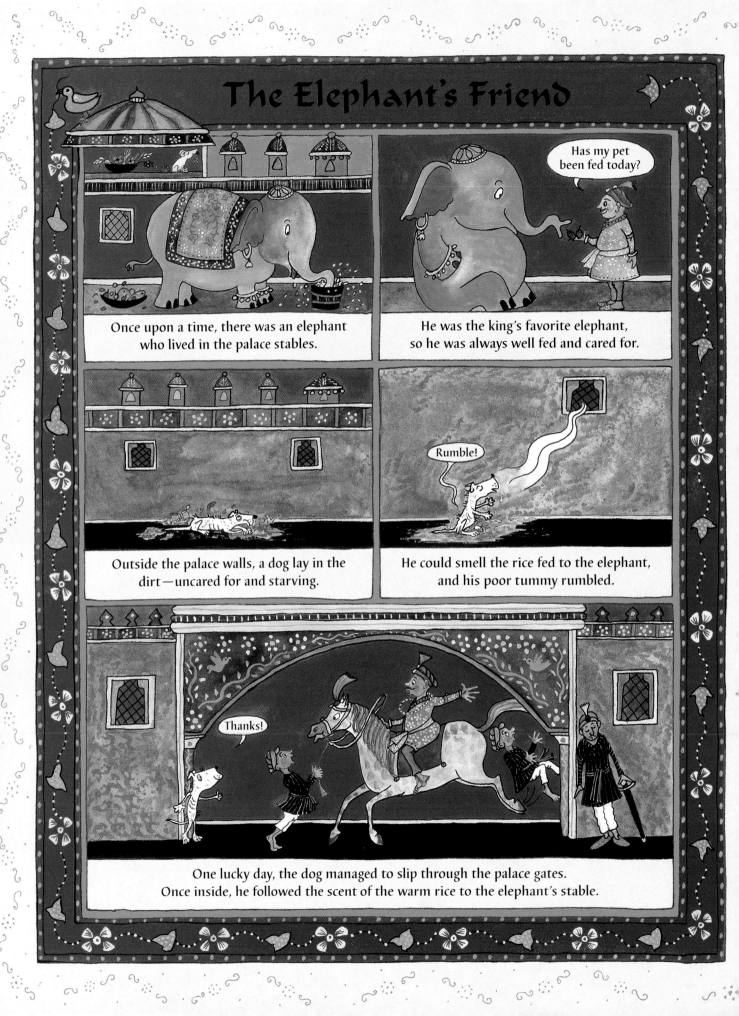

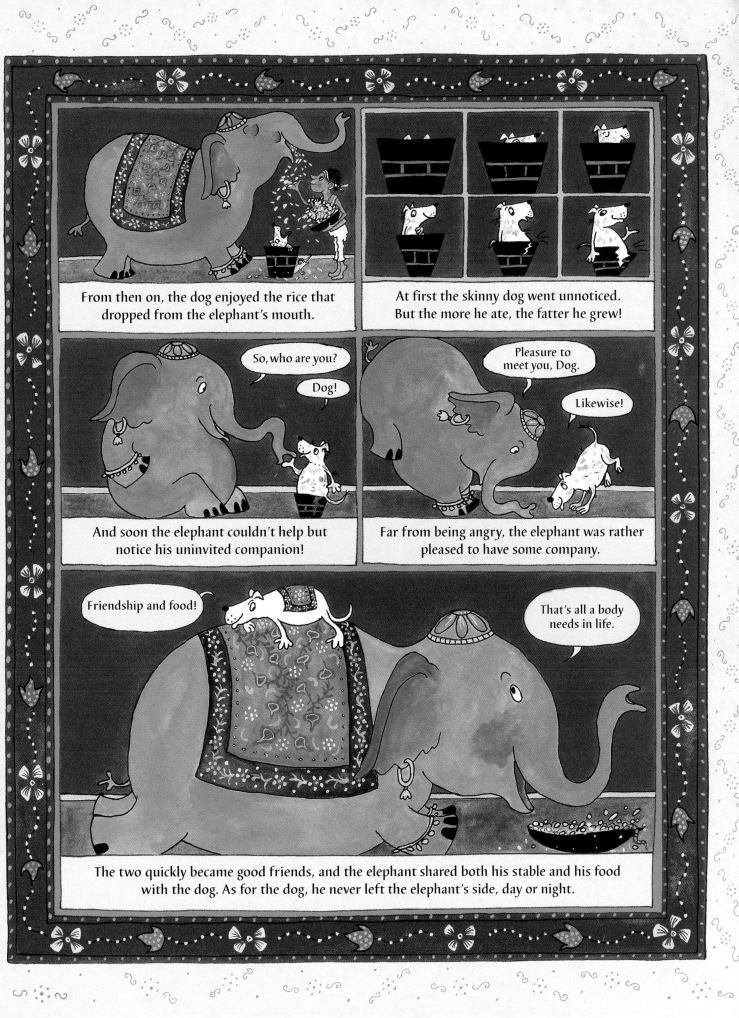

Eventually the king's proclamation reached the village where the dog and the merchant lived. The threat of punishment really scared the merchant, so he chased the dog out of his yard and down the hill. With his tail wagging all the way, the dog ran helter-skelter back to the elephant.

The elephant and the dog danced with delight while the king, his ministers, and the elephant's keeper all cheered and clapped. And so the two friends lived contentedly together for the rest of their days, and nobody, but nobody, ever tried to part them again!

The Talkative Tortoise

There was once a very talkative tortoise named Kambugriva.

He lived by a pond in the Himalayan Mountains with two geese, Sankata and Vikata.

Silence can be golden!

All might have been well if some villagers hadn't spotted them. The villagers burst into laughter at the sight of two geese carrying a tortoise. Kambugriva was furious! He opened his mouth wide to admonish the villagers and fell tumbling from the sky.

Poor Kambugriva he was never, ever heard from again!

The Wise Little Pebet

All her sons soared into the sky except the very youngest, who failed to take off.

He tried and he tried and he tried, but he just couldn't make it.

So Little Pebet was caught in the claws of the hungry cat! The cat was just about to pop Little Pebet into his mouth when Mother Pebet suggested he would taste better if his sticky feathers were washed.

The Golden Swan

Once upon a time, there was a swan with feathers made of the purest gold.
The swan lived on a fine pond and was rich in both food and friends.

Close by the pond, there lived a poor mother with her two daughters.
Their clothes were rags, their food meager, and their luxuries nonexistent.

The swan felt sad that they had so little and he had so much.

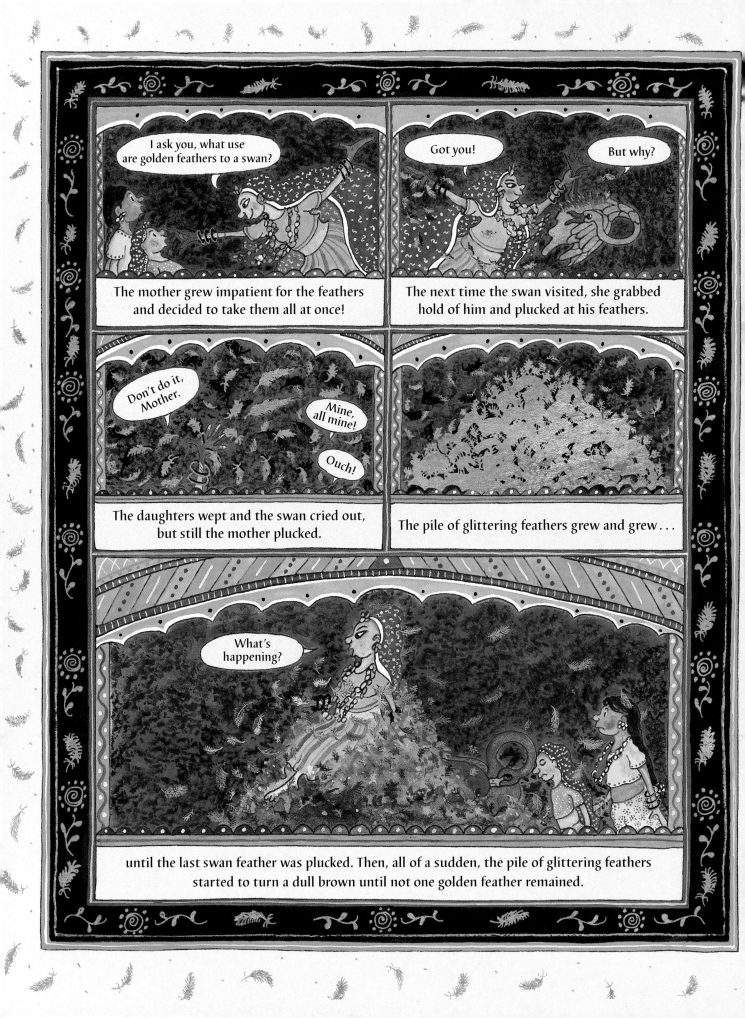

The mother and her daughters gasped in horror, but it was too late. The swan took his leave of the ungrateful woman, who had returned his generosity with such greed. He went with his friends to live in a far distant land, never to return to the little shack again.

The Monkey and the Crocodile

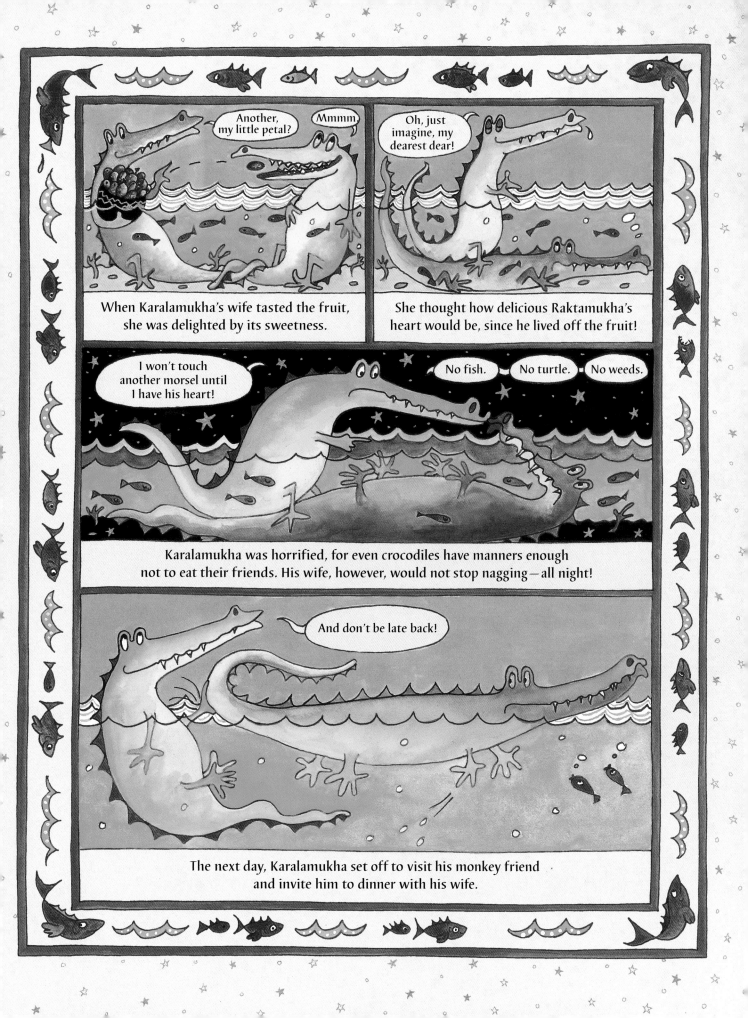

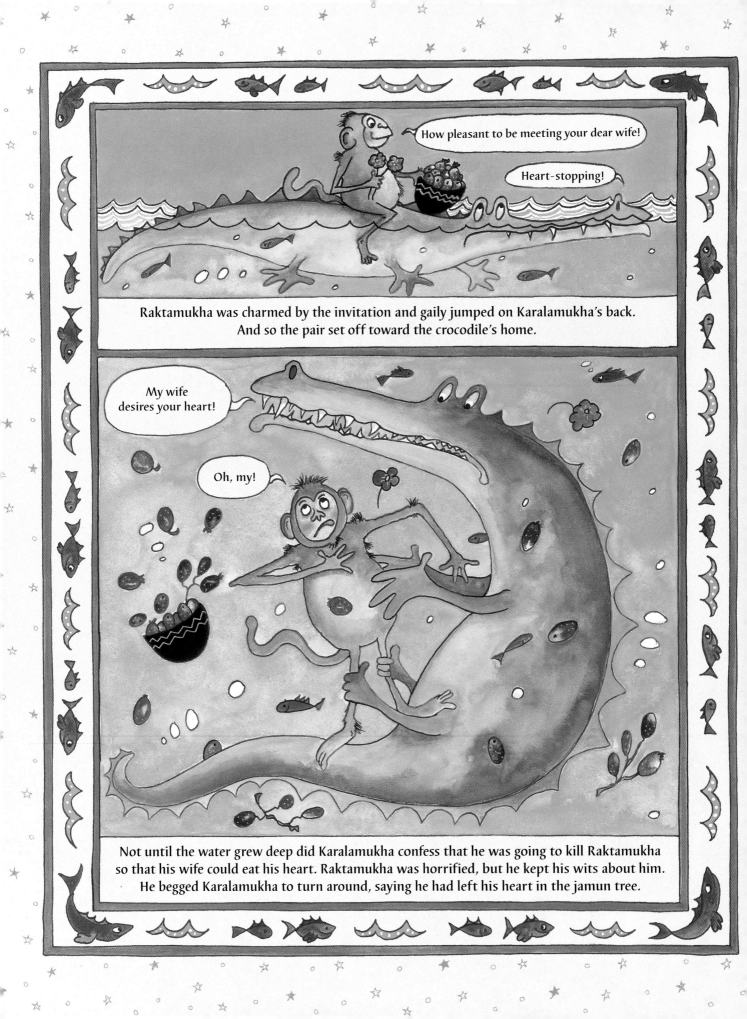

Raktamukha was charmed by the invitation and gaily jumped on Karalamukha's back.
And so the pair set off toward the crocodile's home.

Not until the water grew deep did Karalamukha confess that he was going to kill Raktamukha so that his wife could eat his heart. Raktamukha was horrified, but he kept his wits about him. He begged Karalamukha to turn around, saying he had left his heart in the jamun tree.

The Foolish Lion

In the middle of a forest, there lived an extremely greedy lion named King Bhasuraka.
King Bhasuraka ate at least six forest creatures a day!
He grew fatter and fatter, but the forest creatures grew fewer and fewer . . .

until the animals offered to send one animal a day to King Bhasuraka's den,
to be killed and eaten. Since this would save him from hunting, Bhasuraka agreed.
But he said that if an animal ever arrived late, he would kill all the animals left in the forest!

So every day a forest animal was sent to King Bhasuraka's den, never to return. Bhasuraka found that this system suited him very well and made him feel extremely kingly.

Now, the day came when it was the turn of a wise old rabbit to serve himself up for supper. Old as he was, he was not a bit happy about being eaten. So he hopped very slowly toward Bhasuraka's den, wondering how he might avoid his fate.

By the time Wise Old Rabbit reached the lion's den, Bhasuraka was roaring with impatience. When he saw the skinny old rabbit appear, he roared even louder!

Wise Old Rabbit apologized profusely for his lateness and his smallness. He explained that he had set out with five companions but that another lion, who also claimed to be king of the forest, had eaten them. When King Bhasuraka heard this, he exploded with rage and swore to tear the impostor to shreds!

So that was the end of King Bhasuraka!
Wise Old Rabbit gave a little hop of relief and went to tell his friends the good news.

Although he was old and weak, Wise Old Rabbit became the forest hero,
because he had shown that wisdom can overcome physical strength.

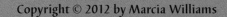

First U.S. edition 2012

Library of Congress Cataloging-in-Publication Data is available.
Library of Congress Catalog Card Number pending
ISBN 978-0-7636-5916-5

12 13 14 15 16 17 CCP 10 9 8 7 6 5 4 3 2 1

Printed in Shenzhen, Guangdong, China.

This book was typeset in Barbedor and Ondine
and hand-lettered by Kate Slater.
The illustrations were done in gouache and ink.

Candlewick Press
99 Dover Street
Somerville, Massachusetts 02144

visit us at www.candlewick.com